علي بابا والاربعين حرامي

Ali Baba and the Forty Thieves

Retold by Enebor Attard

Illustrated by Richard Holland

Arabic translation by Samar Al-Zahar

Mantra Lingua

في قديم الزمان في بلاد العرب، في ليلة مكتملة القمر وهو يجمع الحطب سمع علي بابا صوتاً غريباً جداً، يهدر وكأنة الرعد، لم يأت من السماء ولكن من أعماق الأرض.

A long time ago in Arabia, on a full moon night, Ali Baba noticed something very strange as he gathered firewood. A rumbling sound, like thunder, came not from the sky, but from below the earth.

لدهشة علي بابا، تدحرجت صخرة ضخمة
بنفسها لتكشف عن كهف مظلم.

And to Ali Baba's astonishment, a gigantic rock
rolled across on its very own, revealing a dark cave.

أضفى ضوء القمر ظلالاً غريبةً على امتداد الصخور. أحس علي بابا بأنه لم يكن لوحده وعندئذٍ تسلّل مُقترباً من تلك الظلال ليجد خيولاً في انتظار خيّالتِها. إختبأ علي بابا ولم يمرّ وقت طويل حتى رأى خيالات تلبس عباءات وطاقيات تخرج من الكهف باتجاهة.

The moonlight sent strange shadows across the rocks. Ali Baba felt he was not alone.
He crept closer and nearly fell upon a pack of horses waiting for their riders.
Ali Baba hid and it was not long before a bunch of shadowy cloaks and hoods came
out of the cave towards him.

كانوا لصوصاً في انتظار زعيمهم قائد. عندما ظهر قائد نظر ناحية النجوم ونادى
" سَكِّرْ يا سمسم!"
أهتزت الصخرة الضخمة وببطء تدحرجت الى الخلف لتغلق مدخل الكهف مُخْفية
أسرار الكهف عن العالم بأكمله بإستثناء علي بابا.

They were thieves waiting outside for Ka-eed, their leader.
When Ka-eed appeared, he looked towards the stars and howled out, "Close Sesame!"
The huge rock shook and then slowly rolled back, closing the mouth of the cave,
hiding its secret from the whole world... apart from Ali Baba.

عندما أختفى الرجال عن النظر ، دفع علي بابا الصخرة بكل قوته ولكن
الصخرة ظلت في مكانها وكأنه ليس بإمكان أي قوةٍ في العالم زَحْزَحَتِها.
"إفتح يا سمسم!" قالها علي بابا هامِساً فتدحرجت الصخرةُ ببطءٍ لتُظهرَ
الكهف العميق المُظلِمْ. حاول علي بابا التقدم بهدوء ولكن مع كل خطوة
خطاها صدر صوتٌ عالٍ فارغٌ إمتدت أصداؤه في كلِ مكان. وفجأة تعثر
قدم علي بابا فوقعَ. تدحرج مرّاتَ عديدة حتى إستقرَ على كومةٍ من السجادِ
الحريري المطرز بغزارة. حوله كانت أكياس مملوءة بالذهب وبقطع النقود
الفضية وجرار مملوءة بالألماس والزمرد ومزهريات تحتوي على الكثير
من القطع النقدية الذهبية.

When the men were out of sight, Ali Baba gave the rock a mighty push.
It was firmly stuck, as if nothing in the world could ever move it.
"Open Sesame!" Ali Baba whispered.
Slowly the rock rolled away, revealing the dark deep cave. Ali Baba tried to move
quietly but each footstep made a loud hollow sound that echoed everywhere.
Then he tripped. Tumbling over and over and over he landed on a pile of richly
embroidered silk carpets. Around him were sacks of gold and silver coins, jars of
diamond and emerald jewels, and huge vases filled with... even more gold coins!

"أهذا حلمٌ؟" تساءل علي بابا . تناول قلادةً ألماسية، بريقها آلم عينيه،
إرتداها حول رقبته، ثم ارتدى أخرى وأخرى.عبأ جرابية بالمجوهرات
وملأ كلَّ ُجيوبهِ بالكثيرٍ من الذهب حتى صار من الصعب عليه حتى
الزحف إلى خارج الكهف.
عندما وجد نفسه في الخارج نظر ناحية الكهف وصاح " سكِّر يا سِمسِم!"
فتدحرجت الصخرة لتَسِّد مدخل الكهف.
وكما كان مُتوقعاً، إستغرق على بابا وقتاً طويلاً للعودةِ إلى البيت.
وحين لاحظت زوجته ما كان يحمله بكت من الفَرَحْ حيث أن لديهما
الآن ما يكفيهما طوال العُمْرْ.

"Is this a dream?" wondered Ali Baba. He picked up a diamond necklace and the
sparkle hurt his eyes. He put it around his neck. Then he clipped on another, and
another. He filled his socks with jewels. He stuffed every pocket with so much
gold that he could barely drag himself out of the cave.
Once outside, he turned and called, "Close Sesame!" and the rock shut tight.
As you can imagine Ali Baba took a long time to get home. When his wife saw
the load she wept with joy. Now, there was enough money for a whole lifetime!

وفي اليوم التالي أخبر علي بابا أخاه قاسم بما حدث.
" لا تقترب من الكهف" حذره قاسم " إنه مكانٌ خطير."
هل كان قاسمُ قلقاً على سلامة أخيه؟ لا إطلاقاً.

The next day, Ali Baba told his brother, Cassim, what had happened.
"Stay away from that cave," Cassim warned. "It is too dangerous."
Was Cassim worried about his brother's safety? No, not at all.

وفي تلك الليلة، عندما نام الجميع، تسلل قاسمُ الى خارج القرية ومعه ثلاثةُ حميرٍ. وفي الموقع السحري صاح "إفتح يا سِمسِم!" فتدحرجت الصخرة وانفتح بابُ الكهف. فدخلَ حماران ولكنَ الثالثَ رفضَ التَّحَرُكْ.

جر قاسم الحمار عدة مرات وجلده وصرخ فيه حتى استسلم ودخل الكهف. ولكن الحمار كان غاضباً فرفس الصخرة رفسةً قويةً فتحركت بعنف مُغْلقةً باب الكهف.

" هيًا أيُها الحيوانُ الغبي" زَمجَرَ قاسم.

That night, when everyone was asleep, Cassim slipped out of the village with three donkeys. At the magic spot he called, "Open Sesame!" and the rock rolled open.
The first two donkeys went in, but the third refused to budge. Cassim tugged and tugged, whipped and screamed until the poor beast gave in. But the donkey was so angry that it gave an almighty kick against the rock and slowly the rock crunched shut.
"Come on you stupid animal," growled Cassim.

في الداخل شهق قاسم بمُتعة. بسرعة ملأ الأكياس واحداً بعدَ الآخر وكوَّمها مُرتفعة على الحمير المسكينة. وعندما لم يعد بإمكانه أخذ المزيد قرَّرَ الرجوع إلى البيت.

نادى بصوت مرتفع "إفتح يا كاشيو!" ولكن لم يحدُث شيئاً.

"إفتح يا لوزي!" نادى: لاشيء مرة أخرى.

"إفتح يا فستق حلبي!" ولكن لا شيء.

بدأ قاسم يفقد الأمل، فصرخ ولعن وحاول كل طريقة ممكنة ولكنه لم يتذكر كلمة "سمسم!".

لقد وقع قاسم وحميره الثلاثة في الفخ.

Inside, an amazed Cassim gasped with pleasure. He quickly filled bag after bag, and piled them high on the poor donkeys. When Cassim couldn't grab any more, he decided to go home. He called out aloud, "Open Cashewic!" Nothing happened.

"Open Almony!" he called. Again, nothing.

"Open Pistachi!" Still nothing.

Cassim became desperate. He screamed and cursed as he tried every way possible, but he just could not remember "Sesame"!

Cassim and his three donkeys were trapped.

وفي الصباح جاءت زوجة الأخ وطرقت على باب علي بابا منزعجة.
قاسم لم يعد إلى البيت. قالتها بحزن. "أين هو؟ آه أين هو؟"
صُعِقَ علي بابا للخبر وبحث عن أخيه في كل مكان حتى أنهكه التعب.
أين يمكن أن يكون قاسم يا تُرى؟ وعندئذ تذكر وذهب إلى الصخرة.
وهناك وجد قاسم وجثته مرمية خارج الكهف. لقد وجده اللصوص أولاً.
"يجب أن يُدفن قاسم بسرعة." فكر علي بابا وهو يحمل جسد أخيه
الثقيل إلى البيت.

Next morning a very upset sister in law came knocking on Ali Baba's door.
"Cassim has not come home," she sobbed. "Where is he? Oh, where is he?"
Ali Baba was shocked. He searched everywhere for his brother until he
was completely exhausted. Where could Cassim be?
Then he remembered.
He went to the place where the rock was. Cassim's lifeless body lay
outside the cave. The thieves had found him first.
"Cassim must be buried quickly," thought Ali Baba, carrying his brother's
heavy body home.

عندما رجع اللصوص لم يجدوا جثة قاسم. رُبما أن تكون الحيوانات المتوحشة قد سَحَبَتْه بعيداً. ولكن لمن تكون آثار الأقدام هذه؟

"هناكَ من يَعْرف بسرنا." صرخ قائد بغضب شديد. " هو الآخر يجب أن يُقتلْ."

تتبع اللصوص آثار الأقدام حتى وصلوا إلى موكب الجنازة المُتجهة إلى بيت علي بابا.

"هذا هو بالتأكيد" فكر قاسم، وبصمت رسم دائرة بيضاء على الباب الأمامي.

"سأقتله الليلة والجميع نائمون."

ولكن قائد لم يكن يعلم أن هناك من رآه.

When the thieves returned they could not find the body. Perhaps wild animals had carried Cassim away. But what were these footprints?

"Someone else knows of our secret," screamed Ka-eed, wild with anger. "He too must be killed!"

The thieves followed the footprints straight to the funeral procession which was already heading towards Ali Baba's house.

"This must be it," thought Ka-eed, silently marking a white circle on the front door. "I'll kill him tonight, when everyone is asleep."

But Ka-eed was not to know that someone had seen him.

الخادمة مُرجانة كانت تراقبه. أحست بأن هذا الرجل الغريب شرير. "ما الذي تعنيه الدائرة يا ترى؟" فكرَتْ وانتظرت حتى ذهب قائد ثم قامت بعمل ذكي جداً. أحضرت طباشير بيضاء ورسمت دوائر بيضاء على جميع أبواب القرية.

The servant girl, Morgianna, was watching him. She felt this strange man was evil. "Whatever could this circle mean?" she wondered and waited for Ka-eed to leave. Then Morgianna did something really clever. Fetching some chalk she marked every door in the village with the same white circle.

That night the thieves silently entered the village when everyone was fast asleep.

"Here is the house," whispered one.

"No, here it is," said another.

"What are you saying? It is here," cried a third thief.

Ka-eed was confused. Something had gone terribly wrong, and he ordered his thieves to retreat.

وفي تلك الليلة وعندما كان الجميع نائمين دخل اللصوص القرية بهدوء.

"هذا هو المنزل." همس أحدهم.

"لا بل ها هو." قال الآخر.

"ماذا تقول؟ إنه هنا صاح اللص الثالث."

إلتبس الأمر على قائد وأحس بأن هناك خطأ ما، وأمر لصوصه بالتراجُع.

وفي صباح اليوم التالي عاد قائد ووقع ظلهُ الطويل على بيت علي بابا.
عندئذ تعرَّفَ على الدائرة التي لم يجدها في الليلة السابقة. فكَّرَ بخطة،
سيُقدِمْ إلى علي بابا أربعينَ زيراً جميلاً مُزخرَفاً. ولكن سيكون بداخل
كل زير لصٌّ ينتظرُ وسيفهُ جاهزٌ. وفي وقت لاحق ذلك اليوم دُهشت
مُرجانة لرؤية قافلة من الجمال والخيول والعربات تقف أمام
باب بيت علي بابا.

Early next morning Ka-eed came back.
His long shadow fell on Ali Baba's house and Ka-eed knew that *this*
was the circle he could not find the night before. He thought of a plan.
He would present Ali Baba with forty beautifully painted vases.
But inside each vase would be one thief, with his sword ready, waiting.
Later that day, Morgianna was surprised to see a caravan of camels,
horses and carriages draw up in front of Ali Baba's house.

جاء رجلٌ بعباءة بنفسجية وعمامة رائعةٍ لزيارةِ سيد مرجانة.
"علي بابا" قال الرجل "إنك ذكي فلقد وجدت أخاكَ وحميت جثته من أنياب
الحيوانات المُفترسة. إن هذا فعلٌ شُجاع وأنت تستحقُ مكافأةً.
إن شيخنا سيد كرغوستان يُقدم إليك أربعينَ زيراً مملوءةً بأروعِ جواهرِةِ."
ولعلكم تعلمونَ الآن أن علي بابا لم يكن ذكياً وأنه تقّبَلَ الهدية بابتسامة ريضة.
"أنظري يا مُرجانة. أنظري ما قدمَ إليَّ."
ولكن مُرجانة لم تكن مُطمَئنة للأمر وأحست بأن شيئاً سيئاً سيحدُث.

A man in purple robes and magnificent turban called on
her master.
"Ali Baba," the man said. "You are gifted. Finding and
saving your brother from the fangs of wild animals is
indeed a courageous act. You must be rewarded.
My sheikh, the noble of Kurgoostan, presents you with
forty barrels of his most exquisite jewels."
You probably know by now that Ali Baba was not very
clever and he accepted the gift with a wide grin.
"Look, Morgianna, look what I have been given," he said.
But Morgianna was not sure. She felt something terrible
was going to happen.

"أسرع." قالت مرجانة بعد أن تركهم قائد. "إغل حمل ثلاثة جمال من الزيت حتى يخرج الدخان من الأوعية. أقولُ أسرع قبل فوات الأوان وسأشرح لك لاحقاً." بسرعة أحضر علي بابا الزيت الخام وهو يغلي ويُبقبق نتيجة غليانه بواسطة لهب آلاف قطع الفحم. ملأت مُرجانة دلواً بالزيت الخبيث وسكبته في الزير الأول وأغلقت الغطاء بإحكام. اهتز الوعاء بشدة حتى كاد أن ينقلب. بعد ذلك هدأ. فتحت مرجانة الغطاء فرأى علي بابا لصاً ميتاً! وباقتناعه بالخطة قام علي بابا بمساعدة مرجانة في قتل كل اللصوص وبالطريقة نفسها.

"Quick," she called, after Ka-eed had left. "Boil me three camel-loads of oil until the smoke rises out of the pots. Quick, I say, before it is too late. I will explain later."

Soon Ali Baba brought the oil, spluttering and hissing from the flames of a thousand burning coals. Morgianna filled a bucket with the evil liquid and poured it into the first barrel, shutting the lid tight. It shook violently, nearly toppling over. Then it became still. Morgianna quietly opened the lid and Ali Baba saw one very dead robber!

Convinced of the plot, Ali Baba helped Morgianna kill all the robbers in the same way.

That evening Ka-eed arrived to feast with Ali Baba.
They gorged on meats and breads cooked in wonderful ways.
They drank the rich nectar of sumptuous fruits.
But the highlight was Morgianna's dance! Poor Ka-eed did not
have a chance. Belching with the rich food, his eyes rolled
round and round watching Morgianna spin closer and closer.
Then all of a sudden, he felt a diamond studded dagger plunge
into the depths of his heart.

وفي ذلك المساء وصل قائد ليحتفل بالعشاء مع علي بابا. التهموا اللحوم وأنواع الخبز المُحضَّرة بطرُقٍ بديعة. وشربوا رحيق الفواكهة اللذيذة. ولكن قمة الحفلة كانت رقصة مُرجانة! ولم يكن لدى قائد المسكين أية فرصة للنجاة. مُتجشئًا من الطعام الدسم وعيناه تدوران وهو يشاهد مُرجانة وهي تلف راقصة مُقتربة منه أكثرَ فأكثر.

وفجأة أحسَ بخنجرٍ مُرصع بالألماس يدخلُ في أعماق قلبه.

وفي اليوم التالي رجع علي بابا إلى مكان الصخرة. فرغ الكهف من مُحتوياته
السرية من المُجوهراتِ والكنوز وصاحَ "سكِّر يا سمسم!" للمرة الأخيرة.
وزع الجواهر على أبناء الشعب الذين بدورهم نصَّبوا علي بابا قائداً لهم.
أما مُرجانة فلقد عيَّنَها علي بابا مُستشارتَهُ الرئيسية.

The next day Ali Baba returned to the place where the rock was. He emptied the cave
of its secret coins and jewels and he called out, "Close Sesame!" for the last time.
He gave all the jewels to the people who made Ali Baba their leader.
And Ali Baba made Morgianna his chief adviser.